THE HIST

CAMPING IN
COLORADO

By
DANIEL KENNEY

Published by Trendwood Press

Illustrations by Sumit Roy
Cover Design by BZN Studio Designs
Formatting by Polgarus Studio
Editing by David Gatewood

Contents

1. Hanging On...1

2. Grin And Bear It 17

3. All Aboard 41

4. The Mercedes Crystal 53

5. Operation Mirabel....................................73

6. A New Friend 81

7. A Very Important Secret........................95

8. Avalanche! 105

9. Meet The Parents 115

Books By Daniel Kenney 131

About the Author... 133

COLORADO

Chapter One

Hanging On

We fell and we fell and we fell.

Then suddenly, we landed.

I opened my eyes, but it was dark. "Toad?" I called out.

"Here," said a distant voice behind me.

I spun around. It was still dark, but a sliver of light issued from the end of what I could tell must be some kind of tunnel.

"Toad?" I said again.

"April, we're in a cave. I'm at the entrance."

I had just started to move toward the light when I heard a scream.

"Toad!" I shouted. "What's wrong?"

"It's not me, April. It must be Henry."

At first I laughed, thinking Henry must have just realized that he hadn't eaten in a few hours. But when I heard the second scream, I knew that wasn't the problem at all.

This was the scream of someone who was very scared.

For real.

I scrambled to the mouth of the cave as quickly as I could. The cave opened onto the side of a mountain, and just a few yards ahead of me the ground dropped off. Toad and I were standing just a short way from the edge of the cliff.

Henry screamed again. "Help! April, help!"

The voice was coming from right in front of me.

From below the edge of the cliff.

We ran to the cliff, and I peered over.

Henry was just a few feet below me, clinging to a branch of a tree that had grown out of the side of the cliff. His feet were dangling below him, and the branch was bouncing up and down.

"Henry!" I shouted. "I'm here!"

When he jerked his head up, the branch bounced up and down even worse. I could tell he wanted to look down, but I snapped my fingers at him.

"Henry, don't you dare! Don't you dare look down! Toad and I are going to get you. That branch is strong enough to hold you, but you have to stop moving long enough for us to help."

I peered down the cliff. About twenty feet below Henry was a wide ledge. If, God forbid, Henry fell, I was pretty sure he had enough room to land. But I hoped it didn't come to that.

I stood up and looked around. Another tree stood just a few feet away from me, on the top of the cliff, very near the edge. If I had a rope…

Then an idea came to me. I undid the belt

from my jeans, wound it around the tree, and tied my shoe into it. I told Toad to tighten it.

"Toad, you have to make certain that my foot can *not* come lose from this belt. You understand?"

I inched my belly over the edge of the cliff and reached out my arm.

"Okay, Henry, I need you to move along that branch, toward the cliff, as carefully as you possibly can. I'm tied off so I can't fall. I'm going to grab you with two hands, and you're going to climb up my back. Toad will help you up over the edge of the cliff. Got it?"

"No," Henry said, his face full of a terror I'd never seen from him before. "I don't got any of that."

"Fine, we'll take it one step at a—"

I stopped midsentence because of what I saw on the ledge down below. My heart started beating like mad.

"What is it, April?" Henry asked. "What's wrong?"

But I couldn't tell him. If I told him, then he'd panic, and we'd have zero chance of getting him to safety.

I had to stay calm. It was Henry's only chance.

"Just keep your eyes on me and worry about getting to my hands," I said.

As scared as he was, and as much as I was sure his instincts were telling him to look down, he didn't. But it didn't matter. Because as he inched his way along the branch toward the edge of the cliff, the grizzly bear on the ledge below him stood up on its hind legs and let out an absolutely ferocious roar.

And that's when the tree branch cracked.

Henry screamed and let go—just as I grabbed him with both hands. One hand had him by the shirt, one hand had him by the hair. His weight started pulling me over the ledge, but my shoe got caught in the belt and the tree. Toad had hold of my other leg and I could tell he was pulling with everything he had.

"Grab the branch!" I shouted at Henry.

Henry responded with the loudest scream I'd ever heard.

I didn't know if he screamed because I was ripping his hair out of his head or because a seven-hundred-pound animal was trying to eat him.

I assumed it was a combination of both.

I lifted as hard as I could, the bear still roaring and growling and scraping the air with his giant paws.

Henry's left hand found the branch. That allowed me to let go of his hair and grab hold of his shirt with both hands. I heaved. His other hand found the branch. I still didn't let go of his shirt, and as he moved hand over hand toward the cliffside, Toad was able to pull me backwards onto surer ground. Finally, when Henry was close enough, I reached down and grabbed his belt.

"On the count of three, Henry. One, two, three!"

Toad pulled me, I pulled Henry, and Henry grabbed hold of the ledge and heaved himself upward.

A moment later we found ourselves tangled up in one big heap.

"Did you really have to hold on to me by my hair?" Henry said.

"Did you really want me to let the bear eat you?"

"I see your point, honestly I do. But April, have you ever been held in the air by your hair?"

"For the sake of ending this discussion, I will admit that no, I've never done that."

"Then thank you for not letting the very angry bear eat me. Although, if he had, the joke totally would have been on him."

"Why?"

"Look at me. Do you really think I would taste very good?"

"You do have a peculiar odor."

Henry made a face. "I know, right? My odor is the worst."

I noticed Toad was being quiet, which wasn't all that unusual. He was on his belly, and he was peeking over the edge of the cliff.

And then I noticed something else.

The bear was quiet, too.

"April," Toad said. "I think we have a problem."

"What?"

Toad turned around. "The bear? She's gone."

I slithered on my belly to join Toad. Sure enough, there was no bear in sight.

I pointed to a cave on the ledge down below. "She must be in her cave."

Toad shook his head and pointed the other direction. "She ran that way."

"Why?"

He shrugged and turned his tiny face my way. "I think she's coming for us."

He said it so casually that, for a moment, it didn't register.

And then it did. I looked in the direction that

Toad had pointed. The ledge narrowed into a trail, a trail just wide enough for a bear, and hugged the rock cliff for some distance.

Henry joined us. "But she can't get up that cliff."

Toad shrugged again. "I think she knows another way up here."

I closed my eyes and listened. To the sound of birds behind me. To the soft whoosh of the wind through the trees to my left. And somewhere to my right, in the distance, was the faint but unmistakable roar of a very large and very angry bear.

I jumped to my feet and pulled Toad with me. "Come on, Henry, let's run!"

The three of us sprinted to our left, through the woods, having absolutely no idea where we were going. And frankly, I didn't care. I just wanted to put as much distance between us and that bear as possible.

After a few minutes, poor Toad's face looked like it was going to explode. So we stopped, and Toad fell to the ground and tried to catch his breath.

"Think we're out of the woods yet?" Henry asked.

I looked around at the dark canopy of trees that surrounded us. "No, we're still in the woods."

"I meant did we lose the bear?"

I laughed. "I know what you meant." I closed my eyes to listen to the sounds again. The first thing I heard was the crack of a branch followed by a bear's mighty roar. And this roar wasn't at all faint.

"Run!"

I grabbed Toad's hand, and we booked it through the woods. The roars were getting louder, and the trees and branches behind us snapped like some giant machine was making its way through the forest.

Ahead of us was a break in the trees. I could see blue sky and sunlight. I burst through the trees first and put on the brakes as soon as I realized where we were. I stopped Toad short and put out my hand and yelled for Henry to stop.

Now I knew why the trees had thinned and the sky had opened. We were at the edge of another cliff. And this one dropped fifty feet to a white-capped river below.

"April!" cried Toad. "What are we going to do?"

"I don't suppose we could just reason with the bear, could we?" asked Henry.

The bear let out its loudest roar yet, and a shiver ran down my back that made every hair on my body stand on end.

I turned around. Behind us, something strange was happening with the green forest. The leaves were bending, as if the forest was moving.

It was.

I turned back to the river and checked for the book. It was still tucked into the front of my pants and under my shirt. I looked over the edge of the cliff at the water below.

I gulped.

"Henry, we don't have much of a choice."

He looked down at the river and then at me, his eyes wide with fear. "You sure I couldn't try to reason with it? I know a thing or two about being hungry. Maybe the bear and I could become friends."

The mighty grizzly burst through the trees behind us.

The three of us did two things in unison.

We screamed.

And we jumped.

I let go of Toad's hand in midair, and as I looked to the water below, I prayed that we didn't hit any rocks.

When I finally hit the water, the impact made it *feel* like I'd hit a rock. Water rushed up and into my eyelids. The rapids tumbled me sideways beneath the water, and I couldn't tell up from down. I was looking, trying to find Toad, but I couldn't see anything but white bubbly water.

At some point, my hip slammed into a rock, and that tossed me yet again. I was running out of breath, and I remembered what my dad had once taught me. *Swim with the current.* So that's what I did.

I swam with the current, no longer worrying about getting to the surface. I swam, and then I took a sharp left and started swimming to what I hoped was the riverbank. Before I knew it, my feet touched the bottom. I jumped out of the water and took the biggest breath of fresh air I'd ever taken. My chest heaved.

Toad was lying on his back on the riverbank in front of me. From farther upstream, Henry was walking toward us holding his side.

"Are you both all right?" I asked.

Henry had his shoe off and was pouring water out of it. A little fish swam out. I saw Henry look at it. I knew that look. He was wondering if he should eat it.

Toad rolled onto his belly and started scurrying about the ground, looking for critters.

I let out a big breath of relief. It looked like everything was back to normal.

I checked my belly. The book was right where I'd left it.

Which meant it was time to figure out exactly where we were.

CHAPTER TWO

GRIN AND BEAR IT

In my sopping wet clothing, I sat down on a rock and took out the book. I looked around at the river, the mountains, the forest, and tried to imagine where we might be.

Henry was clearly doing the same thing. Then his eyes lit up and he snapped his fingers.

"Before you open up the book, I say we guess. Toad, which state do you think we're in?"

Toad picked up a pebble and threw it into the river. Then he looked my way. "Montana."

"Okay, short stuff votes Montana. April, what say you?"

"That was a pretty big bear back there. I'm going with Alaska. How about you, Henry?"

"Well, we are without a doubt in the middle of a wilderness. And we practically died trying to get through it. I'm voting my room."

"Your room?"

"Have you ever seen my room? I've got stacks of dirty underwear in there taller than some of those trees, and one time I tried to get to my bathroom and I got trapped in a broken laundry basket. That was one scary night. Thankfully, I found a half-eaten ham sandwich on the floor so that eased my suffering."

Toad gave me a pained expression. "Does he ever stop talking?"

I shook my head and laughed. "Only when his mouth is completely full. Okay, Montana, Alaska, and Henry's bedroom. Let's see who won."

I set the book on my lap. As usual, a shape was magically carved into the book's thick cover. The one looked kind of like a rectangle.

And I knew of only two states that had a shape like that.

I opened the book. A map of the state was on the left-hand page, and on the right was a list of state facts labeled, "The Colorado File."

Colorado

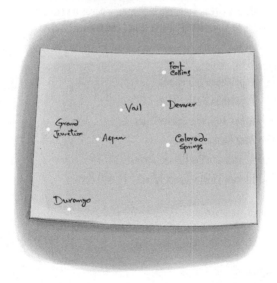

The Colorado File

Located on the eastern edge of the Western United States, Colorado encompasses most of the southern Rocky Mountains and the western edge of the Great Plains. Named for the Colorado River, the state is a tourist attraction for outdoor enthusiasts from around the world who travel to Colorado to enjoy hiking, climbing, fishing, kayaking, and skiing. The state is home to world famous ski resorts such as Aspen, Vail, Telluride, Breckenridge, Beaver Creek, Steamboat, and Copper Mountain. The capital and most populous city in Colorado is Denver, a major US city and home to professional sports teams and major industry.

State Capital: Denver
Population: 5,540,545
Population Rank: 21st
Area: 104,094 Square Miles
Area Rank: 8th
Admitted to the Union: August 1, 1876
Highest Point: Mount Elbert - 14,440 Feet

"We were all wrong," I said. "We're in Colorado!"

I glanced over the map and the Colorado File quickly, then moved on to the next page, where a date had appeared.

July 25, 1850

"Today is July 25, 1850," I said.

"And what was so special about July 25, 1850 in Colorado that our magical book had to send us through history?"

That was the question. If we'd learned one thing with our limited experience in traveling history, it was this: figure out what's important about the date in history, find the crystal map piece, and move on.

Hopefully to a time when we could travel back home to New York with our father.

I thumbed through the book, skimming important dates in Colorado's history.

In 1803, the US acquired a territorial claim to the Eastern Rocky Mountains and what would become Colorado through the Louisiana Purchase that Thomas Jefferson negotiated with Spain.

Spring of 1833, fur trader William Bent establishes Bent Fort, the first American

establishment in the future state of Colorado, along the bank of the Arkansas River. Bent would destroy the fort in 1849.

On April 9, 1851, the first permanent European-American settlement in the future state of Colorado was established at San Luis de la Culebra.

On February 28, 1861, US President James Buchanan signed an act of Congress organizing the free territory of Colorado.

On August 1, 1876, Colorado became the thirty-eighth state in the Union.

"Guys, I think we have a problem."

I thumbed back through the history to be sure. But between William Bent destroying his own fort in 1849 and San Luis de la Culebra being established in 1851, there was nothing.

"I have no idea what happened on today's date."

"What do you mean you have no idea?" asked Henry.

"I mean, it's not here. There is no July 25, 1850."

"Is that part ripped out?"

"No, it's not ripped out. I'm telling you, it's just not here."

"But that doesn't make sense," said Henry. "I thought the book was supposed to lead us to the puzzle piece. How will we know what to do if we don't even know what happened on this date in history?"

"Henry, I have to be honest. That's the most well thought-out question I've heard you ask since, well, probably forever. Usually, all you talk about is food."

"It's sad, isn't it? I think all this time travel is messing with my brain."

"You mean it's making you smarter?"

He shrugged. "Like I said, sad."

"But back to your point about the book leading us… that *is* what Dad and Benjamin said. So why would the book send us to a day when nothing important happened?"

Toad stood up and shook his head. "Just because history doesn't record what happened on this day doesn't mean nothing important happened."

"What do you mean?" I asked.

"I don't think this has anything to do with an important event in history. I think it's got something to do with that bear."

"The bear who tried to eat us? *That* bear."

"That's my point. Why did she attack us?"

"Because Henry almost plopped down in front of her cave. My guess, she's got cubs in there."

Toad scratched at his chin. "Okay, let's say you're right. Then once we got Henry back to the cliff, why didn't the bear leave us alone?"

"Because she was mad," I said.

"She was mad that we threatened her cubs… so she leaves her cubs and goes way out of her way to get back up to the cliff and attack us?"

"What are you getting at, Toad?"

"Maybe she *wasn't* trying to attack us."

"Well if she wasn't trying to attack us, what *was* she trying to do?"

Before Toad could respond, a noise rang out from above the river: a loud, long howl. Not an angry roar. More of a long bellow.

Toad's eyes traced the river back to the spot where we'd jumped in. "I think that bear needs our help."

And with that, Toad started walking.

Henry gave me a bewildered look.

"The bear needs *our* help?"

I shrugged. "That's what Toad thinks."

"The bear who was ready to swallow me whole. *That* bear."

"Did you see any other bear up there?"

I jogged ahead to catch up with Toad, and Henry joined us a moment later.

"Listen, Toad," said Henry. "I know I've made a lot of cracks about your short legs and the occasional crack about your obsession with creepy crawly things... but do you mind telling me why we're walking back the way we came?"

"Because this is the way to the bear."

"I was afraid you were going to say that. Um,

Toad, do you have experience talking to bears that I should know about?"

"Nope."

"So, do you plan on just calling him Mr. Bear?"

"I'm pretty sure she's a girl."

"Okay… Then do you plan on talking to *Mrs.* Bear and just asking her why she appeared to be attacking us?"

"April," Toad said. "Henry knows bears can't talk, right?"

I looked at Henry and smiled. "Did you know that, Henry?"

"Yes, of course I know that bears can't talk."

Toad stopped at a part of the cliff that was more like a really steep hill. He grabbed on to a tree root and wedged his foot into another one. "The climbing shouldn't be too bad here."

Henry looked at me with crazy eyes. Then he put one hand over the other and made a pretend whistle sound with his mouth. "Okay, time out. Time out. The fun's over. You both had me, you really did. Oh, we're going to go help the nice old grizzly bear. That will be a scream, watching Henry get all scared."

"Henry," I said, "I don't think Toad is joking."

Henry threw his hands into the air. "Then I really do *not* understand what we're doing."

Toad rolled his eyes like he was getting quite annoyed, then he turned away from the hillside, faced Henry, and took a breath.

"It's really quite simple. You said it yourself. The book leads us to where it wants us. Yes, nothing 'important' happened in history today... but it doesn't matter, the book takes us to where the missing puzzle piece is. And the book not only led us to Colorado on this day, it led us to *that bear*. But, as we have all now agreed, bears can't talk. They don't know how to ask for help. You know what they do instead of talking? They roar. And the reason she came after us even though we were safely away? She didn't want us to leave. My guess is she does have cubs and she needs our help."

"So, even if you're right about all that," Henry said, "what exactly is your plan?"

Toad shrugged. "Climb up to that ledge and help her."

And with that, Toad grabbed onto the root and began climbing. The ledge was forty feet above us, but Toad took a zigzag route that allowed him to get up there without having to do any serious climbing.

"April! This is your oldest friend Henry speaking. You know the one who really likes food… but doesn't like to *be* food? You see, there's a real difference between the two. For one, when you become the food… you're dead."

"I get the concept, Henry, but I think Toad's right."

"You think he's right? April, this isn't a game show. If we get the wrong answer, we don't lose a little bit of money and fun prizes."

"Like I said, Henry, I understand the risk.

But what would you have us do instead? Wander around hundreds of square miles of wilderness just hoping to bump into a small piece of crystal?"

"At least tell me you've got a backup plan for when we get up there and the bear *does* in fact try to eat us?"

I looked up at the cliffs on either side of the river. Then I looked at the wild white river charging past. We didn't have many options. "We could jump into the river," I said.

"We already did that once."

I winked. "And look how well that worked for us."

I grabbed hold of the tree root and pulled myself up. Toad and his little legs were struggling to make it up the zigzag trail, but by gosh, he was doing it. I had to give it to Toad. He might be my little brother, but he had courage. And when it came to animals, he knew more than anybody I'd ever met. That was the only reason I was following him up this steep hillside. I trusted him. I actually trusted him.

I heard Henry scrabbling up the trail behind me, grumbling the whole way. "Do you think that bear woke up this morning thinking, I wonder if I get to eat three little kids today? Probably not. Hey, how do you think she likes her Henry? Medium or medium rare? With all the food I've consumed in my young life, I'd like to think I would be pretty tasty. Gosh, I hope I don't taste like chicken. I mean, whenever you say something tastes like chicken it really means that it tastes like nothing. How depressing would that be to be eaten by a bear and all the bear can say is wow, this Henry tastes just like chicken."

I allowed Henry's voice to fade into background noise as I focused on scaling the hillside.

When I finally reached the top, Toad was peering upward. The very top of the cliff, the place where we started this adventure, was another twenty feet above us.

"What do you see?" I whispered as I came up behind him.

"The mama bear's still up there, probably looking for us."

"Anything else?"

Toad smiled. "Just listen."

I listened. I could hear the mama bear grunting and making a racket as she grumpily made her way through the forest above us.

And then I heard something else. Much closer. It was soft, like a whimper.

It was coming from inside a cave that was positioned on the ledge.

The bear's cave.

"Is that a cub?" I asked.

Toad nodded.

"So you were right?"

"I'm always right about animals."

Henry pulled up alongside us. "Yes, squirt, and you never forget to mention it either. So, Mama Bear's up in the forest trying to find us, Baby Bear's in the cave in trouble. What's the plan here?"

Toad took one look around, then jogged along the ledge and into the cave.

Henry looked at me. "The plan is to just walk into a grizzly bear's cave and wing it? We've got to talk to Toad more about the whole concept of a plan."

Henry and I followed Toad toward the whimpering of what I really hoped was a small and very cute cub.

Inside the bear cave, the air smelled different. Like a combination of wet dog and something else. Something bad. Henry pointed to the far wall, and there, at its base, was the mostly eaten carcass of what I was guessing had once been a deer. But the smell and the carcass didn't seem to faze Toad. He kept moving through the cave.

And then all of a sudden he stopped.

"The little guy's definitely hurt," he called from up ahead.

Toad was kneeling down next to a bear cub. The cub was on his side, writhing about and whimpering in obvious pain.

But now that we were there, he was doing something else, too. He was growling and snapping his jaws, doing his best to be fierce. Still, you could tell the poor little guy's heart wasn't into it.

Toad put one hand on the cub's fur and made a shooing sound with his mouth. When the bear had stopped snapping his jaws, Toad said, "Now don't you worry, little fella. We're going to find out what's wrong, and we're going to help you."

Toad ran his other hand down the little bear's legs until he came to the paw. When he did, the little cub shook wildly, but Toad kept his other hand firmly on the bear's chest and kept making comforting sounds.

That's when I saw it. Sticking out of the fleshy part of the little cub's paw was a very sharp and painful looking thorn.

Toad pointed at it. "I'm sure the mama tried, but she just wasn't able to get it out."

"What do we do?" Henry asked.

"We're getting this thorn out, that's what. April, I'll keep the bear calm. Henry, when I tell you to, you hold his legs still. April, do you think you can grab that thorn and pull it out?"

"But if a giant grizzly bear isn't able to pull it out, what chance do I have?"

"A pretty good chance, considering that you have a very important item that a grizzly bear does not: an opposable thumb. Strangely enough, pandas have opposable thumbs, too. Not quite like ours of course, but much better—"

"Toad!"

He stopped in midsentence. "Sorry, I get excited when I get to talk about animal stuff. April, you'll be able to do this."

I nodded, though I felt more than a little skeptical. The thorn looked like it was stuck really deep inside the cub's paw, and the little guy was obviously in terrible pain.

Toad positioned himself over the top of the bear, continuing to stroke his fur and make calming noises with his mouth. Then Henry positioned himself near the little cub's legs. I knelt next to Henry, took a deep breath, and readied my hands.

"Okay," said Toad. "One, two, three!"

As Henry pinned down the cub's legs, I grabbed the thorn with the tips of my fingers and pulled with everything I had. The bear let out the loudest and most horrible squeal I had ever heard in my life.

"Pull it, April!" said Toad.

I kept yanking, but I felt like I'd need pliers to pull that thorn out. It was lodged down there incredibly deep. The cub kept wiggling back and forth and screaming and howling like nothing I'd ever heard in my life. The poor little cub was in a ton of pain, and I was the cause of it.

And that's when I heard the only thing worse than the sound of that poor cub screaming.

A roar.

That was the most terrible sound I'd ever heard in my life.

It was loud.

It was ferocious.

And it was coming from *inside the cave*.

Fear shot down my spine and gave me the extra bit of juice I needed. I yelled as I gave that thorn one more pull. And then boom… just like that…

The thorn popped out.

The little cub screamed one more time, and then immediately his voice changed. He began merely whimpering instead of howling, and his body stopped shaking.

Mama Bear, on the other hand, wasn't done roaring. And now she was coming for us.

Henry, Toad, and I all let go of the little cub and crouched behind him, trembling. The mama bear rose up on her hind legs, pawing at the sky and roaring. She was absolutely enormous.

I knew this was going to be it for us.

That's when the little bear cub popped up and hobbled over to his mother like nothing had happened. He waited for his mama to lower her head, then the little cub licked his mom's face and buried his little head into her neck.

"He's telling his mom we're all right," explained Toad, like he was narrating a documentary. "He's telling her that we helped him."

Henry leaned in. "Or maybe he's telling his mom he thinks the tall one tastes like chicken. Ever think of that?"

That's when some of the light from outside illuminated something at my feet. It was right where the little cub had been lying. It looked like a piece of glass.

I let out a gasp. "The puzzle piece!"

I moved slowly to grab it, not wanting to startle the bears. I wrapped my hand around the piece and looked at both Henry and Toad.

Toad smiled. "You see? Just like with the alligator."

Henry smiled as well. "I love it when a plan comes together."

Then he did something else.

Something he shouldn't have done.

He clapped his hands together.

The noise echoed off the cave walls. The little cub shrieked, and the mama bear reared up on her hind legs and roared her loudest roar yet.

She charged.

I grabbed the book from my pants, screamed for Henry and Toad, and slammed the puzzle piece into the book's cover, right inside the carved shape of Colorado. Light shot out from the book as I opened it, and Henry and Toad thrust their hands in just as the mighty bear leapt for us.

The scene in front of us froze.

The picture of the mighty bear and her cub and the cave folded back like the page of a book.

Everything went black.

And we started to fall.

CHAPTER THREE

ALL ABOARD

It was dark, and I was falling. I screamed. So did Henry and Toad.

We fell and we fell and we fell.

Then suddenly, we landed.

My face was pressed into something, and when I lifted my head, I saw it was a black suitcase. I turned around to find a rather perturbed man looking down at me.

"This isn't a bed, young lady."

He held up the end of his shoe, pressed it into my side, and kicked me over. I rolled off the suitcase and in front of a woman in a long blue dress.

She stepped over me. "My word!" she said with a fright. "This is not a barnyard!"

Fortunately, the book was in my hand. I scrambled to my feet, stuck the book in the front of my pants, and jumped out of the way of an older couple coming straight for me with suitcases in their hands.

They both looked at me like I was lost, which of course was true. I got out of the way and spun around, trying to get my bearings.

I was in a train station. Nicely dressed men and women walked busily up and down the brick aisles. The men almost all wore hats, those fancy derby hats that I'd seen in so many old movies. The women wore sophisticated dresses, gloves, and heels. Everyone looked so pretty and proper. And everyone looked to be in a hurry.

"April!" said Toad as his little face found me. He jogged toward me.

"Where's Henry?"

Toad pointed. Thirty feet away, Henry was

standing, motionless, in front of a hot dog stand.

"What's he doing?" I asked.

"He's just been standing there, not moving a muscle, like a statue."

"None of our time travels have plopped us down in front of a hot dog stand before. I suppose he's just in shock."

"Should we throw an ice-cold bucket of water on him?" Toad smiled. "It's what they do in the movies."

"That would be fun. No, I suppose we should figure out what we're doing in a train station first."

"Do we just leave him there?"

"He might get arrested for creepiness. Let's get him."

Toad and I weaved through the crowd to our statue-like friend.

"Whatcha doing, Henry?"

"Can you smell it, April? Those are hot dogs. Hot dog stand hot dogs. Like back home in

New York. But somehow, these smell even better."

"You know we don't have any money to buy you a hot dog."

"I was hoping if I looked desperate enough, the hot dog guy might just give one to me."

The vendor was a rough-looking man with three chins, a five o'clock shadow, and a half-eaten cigar sandwiched between large yellow teeth.

I leaned toward Henry. "He doesn't look like much of a softie. Come on, big guy. Let's figure out where we are."

We found a bench and sat down. I pulled the book out and opened it up. The map of Colorado was still on the left, and "The Colorado File" was on the right. I turned the page.

On the top was the same date, July 25, 1850, a date completely unimportant in Colorado history—but a day *very* important to a mama grizzly bear with a very hurt cub.

Underneath that date was a new date.

October 23, 1936

"Okay, guys," I said. "Today is October 23, 1936."

Henry snapped his fingers. "Well, we know something about 1936."

"What's that?" asked Toad.

"They have very good smelling hot dogs in 1936."

I frowned, and Henry tilted his head and gave me a sassy look. "Oh, like *you* know something about 1936?"

"I know that Jesse Owens won four gold medals at the 1936 Olympics in Berlin."

"Who the heck is Jesse Owens?"

"Seriously? Do you ever pay attention during school?"

Henry leaned down to Toad. "This is a trick question, right?"

I shook my head. "For your information, Jesse Owens is one of the greatest athletes of the twentieth century. And a trailblazer. He was an African-American athlete who went into Adolf Hitler's home stadium in Berlin and was the best athlete at those 1936 Olympics. He won four gold medals. Four!"

"Geesh, didn't mean to upset you. How on Earth do you know stuff like that?"

"Well, among other things… in case you haven't noticed… *I* am African-American! Then there's that little bit about me being the daughter of a history professor."

"Oh, right, that makes sense. So, Professor April Jefferson, what happens on October 23? Or is the answer that nothing happened on October 23 and we've got to help a giant squid before we can get the puzzle piece?"

"A giant squid?"

"I'm not sure what kind of animal lives in a train station… so I went with giant squid."

I flipped through the book to the section on 1936. Then I flipped through some more until I reached October.

"Okay, got it!" I said. "On October 23, 1936,

the Denver Zephyr took a special nonstop train ride from Denver to Chicago. They covered the 1017 miles in a record twelve and a half hours."

I looked at the others. "Well, it's pretty clear what history wants us to do."

"It really, really wants us to eat one of those super tasty smelling hot dogs?"

"No. The book brought us to a train station. And on this day in Colorado, a train left from Denver and went someplace really, really fast."

"Which means?" said Henry.

"Which means we've got to find ourselves the Denver Zephyr."

We walked down the train platform while I continued to read more about our most recent time travel stop. "Listen up. Denver was founded in 1858. Most of the city sits at an elevation above 5280 feet, leading to its nickname: 'the Mile High City.' And in recent years, Denver's population has made it the nineteenth largest metropolitan area in the United States and the seventh largest metro area in the Western United States."

"Does it say anything in there about them serving delicious hot dogs inside the trains?"

I looked up. We were on a platform between two trains—both of them large, black, and dirty. The way you usually think of trains. But there was another train up ahead of us, on a third track, that was different. It was a gleaming silver and was shaped more like a bullet than a traditional train. A mass of people was gathered around it.

Henry pointed at it. "You know, that one sort of looks like a hot dog."

"I think we just found the Zephyr."

We walked up to the train just as a distinguished-looking man with a silver mustache and a gray tweed suit stepped up onto a wooden crate and hushed the crowd.

"Welcome, welcome," he said. "Many of you have heard of the Denver Zephyr. A few of you have even seen her. But today, a chosen few get to *ride* her… on a particularly special trip. Up till now, the fastest any train has made the trip from Denver to Chicago is in sixteen hours. But we wouldn't expect normal speeds from this shiny silver beast behind me, because the Zephyr is anything but normal. Ladies and gentlemen, we aim to get to Chicago in *under thirteen hours.*"

A gasp rose from the crowd.

"You heard me. Under thirteen hours. How is it possible to go so fast, you ask? Are we strapped down like we're in some sort of race car? Not a chance. We have the latest and greatest diesel engine technology in the world. It's faster, smoother, and quieter than any steam engine you've ever encountered. And in addition to speed, you also get comfort—and, I'll dare say, a bit of luxury. Simply put, the Denver Zephyr is the finest passenger train anywhere in the world. And for the next twelve and a half hours, it's all yours. Step right up with your tickets. Your carriage awaits!"

The crowd pushed forward. I grabbed Toad, and as he and I and Henry escaped to the side, we ran right into a tall, thin man wearing a dark suit.

He looked down at us with a confused expression. "Don't tell me you're the ones Malcolm sent."

"Is there a problem?" I asked.

He rolled his eyes. "He promised me three teenagers. But you're nothing but little kids." He shook his head. "Never mind, I'll give Malcolm a piece of my mind tomorrow. Today, I need you. Uniforms are in the back. Put them on and be ready to work your tails off, got it?"

I looked at Henry, and we both shrugged. Time travel had taught us to go with the flow.

I turned back to the tall man. "We got it, Mister…"

"Posey. Mr. Posey."

"Right. And Mr. Posey, where exactly do we find the uniforms in the back?"

He let out an exasperated sigh. "In the closet next to the bathroom. Now get!"

Posey pointed to a set of stairs near the rear of the train, which we took.

As soon as we had climbed aboard the train, Henry grabbed me.

"April, what exactly is the plan here?"

"Go find the closet by the bathroom, put our uniforms on, and then get to work."

"That sounds a lot like walking into a bear cave with absolutely no clue what we're doing."

"And look how well that turned out."

"You keep using that line. Are you forgetting that a grizzly bear almost ate our faces off?"

"The correct word being *almost*. History led us to Denver, and now it's time to ride the Zephyr. Like the man said, Henry. Our carriage awaits!"

CHAPTER FOUR

THE MERCEDES CRYSTAL

Sure enough, right next to the bathroom was a locker-sized closet with three red and black uniforms. I took the one for girls, and handed the two boy uniforms to Henry and Toad. Henry went into the bathroom and put his on first. He came out looking like a bellhop from the movies.

"I look ridiculous," he said.

"And that's different from normal in what way exactly?" I asked.

Toad was next. Unfortunately, his uniform was way too big for him.

"Don't laugh," he said as Henry started to giggle. "April, I can't wear this."

"I think you sort of have to. Come here." I tucked his overflowing shirt deep into his pants.

"Henry," I said, "do you have a belt?"

"Yes."

"Can Toad borrow it?"

"So *my* pants fall down? Forget it."

"Fine." I searched the closet and found a piece of rope, then threaded it through Toad's pants like a belt. Finally, I rolled up his pants and his shirtsleeves. "There," I said. "That'll work."

"You sure?"

"No, I'm not. It's probably best if you stay invisible."

I slipped into the bathroom, put on my uniform, and came back out.

"You're the only one of us who doesn't look like an idiot," said Henry.

I winked. "So, situation normal then."

"April, what do we do?" asked Toad.

"The man said we're here to work, so… let's find a way to help. If someone gives you an order, do it. And most important of all, find that puzzle piece so we can get off this train."

Mr. Posey entered the train and looked down his nose at us. "Well?" he said.

"Well what?" Henry asked.

"Well get to work!" He pointed at Henry and Toad. "You and you. Get out there and start hauling suitcases inside. And you." He pointed at me. "How good of a waitress are you?"

"Compared to what?"

"Compare to good waitresses." He rolled his eyes, then motioned for me to follow him.

As Toad and Henry scurried off to load suitcases, I followed Mr. Posey into the next car, a passenger car where people were boarding, finding seats, and putting their bags away. We passed right through the car to another car—and this one was definitely not a regular passenger car. It was the dining car. It had a triangular bar on the far side, where a man in a black vest and fancy white shirt was serving drinks.

"Francois," said Mr. Posey. "This is…" He looked at me. "What's your name?"

"April."

Francois squinted at Mr. Posey. "Isn't April a little young to be slinging drinks?"

"That's what I thought too, but that's who Malcolm sent me, and today, I don't have a choice." He turned to me. "Just do what Francois says. And most importantly, keep the customers happy."

As Mr. Posey walked away, Francois handed me an apron, a pad of paper, and a pencil. "Take orders from people. Bring orders to me. Take drinks back to people. Think you can handle that?"

"I think so."

And so, transported through time to a famous Denver train in 1936, I got to work. I went up to people in their seats, asked them for their orders, and wrote down what they wanted. It was actually kind of fun. So much fun, in fact, that I was caught off guard when the train whistle sounded and the train started to pull away from the station. I quickly glanced out the windows, trying to make sure Henry and Toad had gotten back on the train.

I'd just returned from delivering my third tray of drinks when Francois leaned over to me and whispered, "See that couple that just came in?"

At the other end of the car, a man in a gray pinstriped three-piece suit was taking a seat with a woman probably ten years younger than him. She was tall and beautiful, with curly blond hair that fell below her shoulders and rested on what I was guessing was a very expensive brown fur coat.

"That's Mr. and Mrs. Hadley," Francois said. "One of the wealthiest families in all of Denver. We need to give them the best possible service, understand?"

"Understand."

Growing up in New York, you become accustomed to dealing with fancy rich people. People like my father relied on generous donations from the ultra-wealthy to keep their museums and research initiatives going. I never much liked it—but I understood.

I walked over to the Hadleys. Mr. Hadley was looking at the newspaper, while Mrs. Hadley was studying herself in a pocket mirror.

"Excuse me," I said.

The woman turned, and at first I thought she might bite my head off. Then her face relaxed into a warm smile. "You probably need to get us a drink."

"Yes, ma'am."

"You seem young to be a waitress."

"That's what they keep telling me."

"Mr. Hadley will have a bourbon on the rocks."

Mr. Hadley grunted behind his paper. "I would prefer a double."

Mrs. Hadley made a face. "Which is why he'll have a single."

"And for you, ma'am?"

She ran her fingers along a chain that hung around her neck. "Do you have lemonade?"

"We do."

"Then tell the bartender I want just a splash of gin with my lemonade."

As I wrote down her instructions, she grabbed at the chain hanging around her neck and pulled it out from underneath her coat. I gasped when I saw what hung on the end of it. It was clear and sparkly. At first I thought it was a huge diamond, but on second glance, I knew it wasn't. It was a crystal, like one of our puzzle pieces.

Mrs. Hadley saw me staring. "You like?" she said.

"It's beautiful. Is that a crystal?"

"Smart girl. Most people think it's a diamond. But this, this is even rarer than a diamond. It's called a Mercedes crystal."

"I've never heard of a Mercedes crystal."

She winked. "Like I said, they are exceedingly rare. Now remember, just a splash of gin."

I walked back to Francois and handed him the order. That's when I heard a *psssst*. I looked past the bar car to the area that connected the train cars. Henry and Toad were standing there, motioning for me to come join them.

Francois had already made both drinks and was setting them back on the tray. "Order for Mr. and Mrs. Hadley."

"April!" Henry hissed.

I grabbed the tray and walked over to him. "What is it? I've got to deliver these drinks."

"We found the puzzle piece!"

"Already?"

"Our simplest one yet. Toad and I were hauling these really big bags into the baggage car when I dropped one, it opened up, and the piece fell out."

Henry held up the crystal puzzle piece. It

definitely looked like one of our puzzle pieces, but it was hard to see how it would complete the Colorado map. Either there was another piece to the puzzle, or maybe…

I thought of Mrs. Hadley, and a terrible thought crossed my mind.

"Did you say this fell out of someone's suitcase?" I asked.

"Crazy, don't you think?"

"Not crazy," said a voice behind me.

I spun around to find Mrs. Hadley, arms folded, watching us.

"Sounds criminal if you ask me." She turned to Francois. "Bartender, I thought the Denver Zephyr was better than employing thieves."

Francois looked at us. Then he looked back at Mrs. Hadley. "Pardon me, Mrs. Hadley. What are you talking about?"

Mrs. Hadley brushed past me and yanked the crystal out of Henry's hand. "I'm talking about *this*!"

"That's ours!" said Henry.

He leapt toward her. But Francois was too quick. He stuck out his hand, hit Henry in the chest, and stopped him cold.

"What exactly is going on here?" Francois asked.

"Yes," said a brusque voice. Mr. Hadley. He had come up alongside the elegant but very angry woman. His newspaper was at his side. "I'd also like to know what is going on."

"It's these kids," said Mrs. Hadley. "They stole one of my crystals."

"What?" Mr. Hadley said angrily.

"Listen," I said. "I think there's been a mistake."

Mrs. Hadley shook her head. "There is no mistake, I heard it myself. This little thief said he got it from my suitcase. One of the crystals was here around my neck." She pulled it out and showed it to everyone. "And the other crystal was in my suitcase."

Mr. Hadley gave his wife an odd look.

"That's the misunderstanding I was talking

about," I explained. "We also own a crystal, we lost it, and we've been looking for it."

"On the train?" said Francois.

"It's a long story."

"No," said a new figure that had appeared behind Mr. Hadley. "It's an *impossible* story."

It was Mr. Posey. His normally angry expression was now supercharged. "I am going to *kill* Malcolm. Mr. and Mrs. Hadley, I am *so* sorry, and if I could throw these little criminals off the train, I assure you I would."

"You mean you can't?" Mrs. Hadley asked.

"Unfortunately, no. But what I will do is lock them in a private car and guard it until Chicago. Where I will hand them over to the authorities."

"The authorities?" I screeched. "No, Mr. Posey, we're not lying. We lost an important crystal. Not the Mercedes crystal, and I'm sorry for the confusion… but we can't be locked up!"

Mrs. Hadley narrowed her eyes at me. "Then maybe you should have thought about that before you tried to steal my stuff!"

Mr. Posey glared at us and pointed to the back of the car. "Now!"

He escorted us out of that train car, through the next one, and into a third car—a sleeping car. He shoved us into an empty sleeping compartment and fixed me with a cold stare.

"You had to pull something like this? Today of all days?"

"You don't understand," I said.

"You're right," he said. "I don't."

He beckoned down the corridor to another train employee, who came over to join him. This employee wore the same type of uniform as Henry and Toad, but he was older, probably in his twenties, and at least five inches taller than Henry.

"Daniel," said Mr. Posey to the man. "These children are thieves. They are not, I repeat, *not* allowed to leave this compartment."

"What if they have to use the bathroom?" Daniel asked.

"Well…" Mr. Posey hesitated. "We can't very well have them going to the bathroom in the sleeping car. If they must use the toilet, then you will escort them. Understood?"

"Yes, sir."

Mr. Posey gave us a final look of outrage, then stomped away.

The guard entered the compartment with us, shut the door behind him, and looked at us intensely. Then he shrugged, sat against the door, leaned his back against it, and appeared to doze off.

"This is not good," I whispered.

"What are you talking about?" said Henry as he sat down on the cushioned seat that doubled as a bed. "As long as we're locked up in here, they can't make us do any more work. In case you haven't noticed, I'm not a very good employee." He stretched out his arms and laced his fingers behind his head. "I think I might just take a little nap, too."

"Henry, I'm serious! This is not good at all.

The reason the book sent us to October 23, 1936, was to find the missing piece of the puzzle. If we're locked up and get put in jail, we can't do that. And then instead of someday returning to our home in New York, we'll live out our lives in a jail cell somewhere in Colorado."

"Illinois," said Toad.

"What?"

"We might be in Colorado now, but remember we're traveling to Chicago. That's where they'll put us in jail." He shrugged. "But at least I won't be alone."

"That's right, Toad, no matter what happens, we'll always have each other."

I reached my hand out to tussle his hair. But he knocked my hand away.

"I didn't mean you. I meant Mirabel."

I exchanged a look with Henry. "Who's Mirabel?"

Toad reached into his pocket, pulled something out, and showed it to me.

I screamed, which woke the guard, who gave me a dirty look.

"Sorry," I said.

The guard gave me another stink eye before closing his eyes and returning to the land of slumber.

"How long have you had a mouse in your pocket?" I asked Toad.

"About ten minutes."

"And she's already got a name?"

"I make friends easily."

"Where did you find her?"

"While Henry was dropping the woman's suitcase… I noticed the mouse. Naturally, I picked her up, and the rest is history."

"Because that's what every other normal person does when they see a mouse. Pick it up," said Henry.

Toad smiled.

"So, the suitcase you found that crystal in," I said. "Do you think it came from that rich woman?"

"It was a very fancy suitcase," said Henry. "So... probably."

"And what are the chances that we're on this train, looking for a crystal puzzle piece, and some rich snooty lady just *happens* to own a piece of crystal that looks oddly similar to the very puzzle piece we're looking for?"

"Do you think history's got a cruel sense of humor?" Henry asked.

"Under the circumstances? Yes. Yes, I do."

"What now?" Toad asked.

"Well, we're stuck inside a train car, everyone thinks we're criminals, and yet somehow, some way, we've got to take back that crystal puzzle piece. And we've got to do it before this train arrives in Chicago and we're arrested."

Henry shook his head sadly. "There's no way prison food is good, right? I mean, in the movies, it's all slop and gruel. I think I could handle hard time if there were chicken fingers and mashed potatoes, but prison food? I can't do it, April. I just can't do it."

That's when I noticed Toad's eyes. They'd widened, and his mouth had fallen open. Like he'd just figured something out.

He stood up. "April, does your book tell you how far it is from Denver to the Nebraska border?"

"I seriously doubt it."

"Can you guess?"

"I suppose. Why?"

"Just do it, okay?"

So I did. I found the map of Colorado and looked at where Denver was. I found another map with a railroad going straight east toward Nebraska. Then I found the distance across the state of Colorado.

"One hundred twenty-five miles, give or take," I said. "Now why is that important?"

"One more thing. Do we know how fast this train goes?"

"Yeah, the book mentioned that." I flipped back to the section that talked about what the

Denver Zephyr's record-setting trip to Chicago. The trip we were on right now.

"Sixty-five miles an hour… roughly," I said.

"Okay, then that means this train will reach Nebraska a little less than two hours after it departed. How long do you think we've been traveling?"

"I'd guess maybe an hour."

"So would I," Toad said, worry on his face.

"Toad, what on Earth is this all about?"

"I'm not sure… but I've got a bad feeling about this."

"About what?"

"April, I don't think we have until Chicago to find that puzzle piece. I think we only have until we reach Nebraska."

"What do you mean?"

"The book sends us back in history, to a particular state, to find the missing puzzle piece. What happens if we're no longer in that state?"

"I have no idea."

"But it might not be good."

I had a sudden sinking feeling. "I think you're right."

"Which means we don't have eleven hours to get that puzzle piece."

I gulped. "We only have one."

"Exactly," said Toad.

Henry stood up from his seat. "Then it's time for me to take over. What we need is a plan, and I think it's already been established that you two... are *terrible* at plans."

COLORADO

CHAPTER FIVE

OPERATION MIRABEL

It took Henry ten minutes to lay out all the details behind a plan he called "Operation Thunderbolt."

"But we don't have a roller coaster," I said.

"Or a flying dog," added Toad.

"Leave it to you two to try to poke holes in everything," said Henry. "I guess that means we have to go with Plan B."

It took less than a minute for Henry to go over the nuts and bolts of the plan he called "Operation Mirabel."

When he finished, I asked why he didn't just

~ 73 ~

tell us that plan to begin with.

"Well duh, April. Operation Thunderbolt would have been way more cool!"

Even with a simple plan, Toad estimated it had only a twenty percent chance of success. And as we made our final preparations, Henry wondered again what prison food would be like. I seriously hoped that history was on our side.

Operation Mirabel commenced with waking the guard.

"I have to go to the bathroom," I said in the most pathetic voice I could muster.

He looked annoyed.

"I have to go real bad!" I said.

"Fine," he said, "but like Mr. Posey said, you're all going. Now come on!"

I went first, then Toad. Henry hung back in the private car.

"Just a second," he said. "I've got to tie my shoes." As he bent over to tie his shoes, he made sure his belt was in his hands, ready to go.

That's when Toad looked up at the guard. "Could you hold this for me while I go?"

The man leaned over. "Hold what?"

"This!" Toad held out his hands and opened them.

Mirabel jumped out of Toad's hand right onto that poor guard's face. I pushed the man in the chest as hard as I could, and he tumbled over Henry, who was in perfect position. The helpless man fell into the private car, and Henry quickly looped his belt around the man's feet. Meanwhile, Toad leapt on the guard's chest, trying to get Mirabel off, while I used the length of rope to tie the man's hands.

The whole thing took less than thirty seconds, and boy oh boy was that guy mad. And *loud*. We didn't have much time.

Toad scooped up Mirabel, and we stepped out into the corridor and shut the door behind us.

"I'm a little concerned at how good we were at that," said Henry.

"Remember, Henry, that was only phase one. Now the for the hard part. Everyone ready?"

Toad nodded, and Henry saluted.

"And how about you Mirabel?" Toad asked.

I could have sworn she winked.

We took off down that train car and into the next one. We went so fast, I didn't even look to see who noticed us.

I grabbed the book out of my pants and looked at the cover.

"Book is ready. Okay, boys, Henry doesn't like prison food, and I'd hate to see what happens if we reach the Colorado border. We get that crystal puzzle piece, and we get it now."

We burst into the dining car. Francois started yelling as soon as we entered—and he wasn't the only one. But nobody stopped us.

We ran right up to the Hadleys. Both of them were too stunned by our sudden appearance to do anything. But I could see that Mrs. Hadley was guarding something. Her purse.

"We have something for you," I said.

"Oh, I bet you do," she said.

"Show her, Toad."

Toad held Mirabel the mouse right up to that woman's face, and not-so-poor Mrs. Hadley screamed bloody murder and threw her hands into the air.

And in the process, she let go of her purse.

I grabbed the purse and thrust my hand into it

Henry shouted. "April! Bartender's coming!"

Toad was looking in the opposite direction. He shouted too. "Mr. Posey's coming!"

My fingers found the crystal. And as Francois and Mr. Posey closed in on us from opposite sides, I slammed that little crystal puzzle piece into the carved outline of Colorado. Light shot out of the book, like the flash of a giant camera, and everything in the train car started to shake.

"Henry! Toad! Now!"

They both put their hands into the book. And as soon as they did, Francois, Mr. Posey, the Hadleys, and the rest of the passengers froze.

The world in front of us folded back like the page of a book.

Everything went black.

And we started to fall.

COLORADO

CHAPTER SIX

A NEW FRIEND

It was dark, and we were falling.

We fell and we fell and we fell.

Then suddenly, we landed.

I was on my side in a pile of fluffy and very cold snow. The cold jolted me to my senses in a hurry. I tried to get myself out, but my hand plunged deep into the snow and it was hard to find any leverage. I eventually got my footing and was able to get myself upright.

Everywhere around me was more fluffy white snow. And I realized where I was.

I was standing on the slope of a mountain.

And I was very, very cold.

"Where did you come from?"

The voice came from behind me and made me jump out of my skin. I spun around. Just a few feet away stood a girl on skis. She wore a snowsuit, hat, ski goggles, and a big blue backpack. Beside her was an adorable brown and black dog.

"Um, I'm sorry," I said. "I'm looking for my friends."

She slid closer, flipped up her goggles, and studied me with curious blue eyes. Wisps of dirty blond hair ran from under her hat, and she wiped them away from her face. Her dog ran up excitedly and tried to jump up to my arms, but the girl grabbed the dog and pulled it back.

"Sorry about Miley. She's still a pup and she gets excited when she meets someone new. You say you're looking for your friends? On the side of a mountain… without a coat?"

"Y-y-yes," I said. "You haven't by chance

seen a boy, looks like me, only smaller, and a taller, goofy-looking kid?"

"Those are your friends?"

I nodded. And shivered.

"And I'm guessing they don't have coats either?"

I shivered again. "You'd be guessing right."

The girl shook her head and laughed, then unzipped her coat and handed it to me.

"I can't take your coat," I said.

She winked. "You need it more than I do."

"Are you sure?"

"I'm sure that I'm more used to the cold than you. Put it on, and let's go find your friends."

I hesitated, not wanting to let this girl be without her own coat. But the next set of shivers set my teeth to rattling, and I decided to take her up on her hospitality. I slipped the coat on, zipped it up, and hugged myself with my now warm sleeves.

"Thank you very much…"

"Amelia," she answered with a smile. She shot out her hand, and I took it and squeezed. "Amelia Dolan."

"Nice to meet you, Amelia Dolan. My name is April Jefferson."

She looked at me curiously again. Like she and her blue eyes knew something. Then she took off her big backpack and pulled out a pair of snowshoes. "You'll need to wear these, otherwise you won't have much of a chance out here."

She helped me put the snowshoes on. As she did, Miley started to sniff me.

"Is she a German shepherd?" I asked.

"Yep. Only four months old. I got her when she was two days old. Best birthday present ever. And I think she likes you."

That's when Miley stopped sniffing and went into full-on lick mode.

"Miley!" Amelia said. She grabbed the pup and pulled her away. "Give April room to breathe. She doesn't want your nasty dog spit all over her."

I laughed. "I don't mind. She seems nice."

Amelia smiled. "Miley's nice when she has to be, which is most of the time. And then, when it's time to be *not* nice? She can do that pretty well too. She may not be big, not yet. But she's got gumption."

Amelia grabbed me by the hand and helped me to my feet. Then she opened her backpack again, pulled out two more ski poles, and handed them to me. She also pulled out a gray sweatshirt and put it on.

"Wow, talk about prepared," I said.

"I'm the daughter of a mountain man and a competitive snow skier, what can I say? Now, let's go find your friends."

That's when I realized I didn't have everything I needed. I checked the front of my pants, then I fell to the ground and started looking around frantically.

"Did you lose something?" Amelia asked.

"A book."

"You're kidding me."

"No."

"Must be a special book."

"You have no idea."

Amelia knelt down with me, and together we used our poles to dig around in the snow near where I'd landed. Finally, one of my poles hit something. I shot my hand down the little hole I'd created, grabbed the book, and pulled it out.

Amelia craned her neck to get a better look at it.

"That's a weird-looking book," she said. "What's it about?"

"The history of Colorado."

"You must really like history."

"I do."

"Well. Let's find your friends."

Amelia gave me a few tips on using the snowshoes. Once I got started, it wasn't too bad, but it was very slow.

Amelia, on skis, was much faster. She skied on ahead, down the slope, and looked around. She looked back up at me and pointed to the woods. I nodded, angled my snowshoes down a bit, and cut a diagonal across the snow until I met her at the edge of the trees.

"You and your friends from Denver?" she asked.

"Not originally, but that's where we were earlier."

"Did you come to Aspen for the world championship next week?"

Aspen? World championship? I really needed to look at the book and figure out what was going on. But at the moment, all I could do was bluff.

"Yeah. For the championship."

She gave me another one of those curious looks. Then a faint voice sounded from inside the forest.

"Come on!" she said.

She and her puppy raced forward, zigzagging their way expertly through the trees, while I muddled along behind, getting the hang of the snowshoes but still moving slowly. Amelia was nearly fifty feet ahead of me when she shouted to me over her shoulder.

"I think I found them!"

Amelia and Miley vanished, and I followed as quickly as I could.

I reached the spot where she'd shouted, and looked down into a shallow gully. They were all there: Amelia, Miley, Henry, and Toad. Toad had his arms around Miley, while Henry looked like a human Popsicle.

I stepped carefully down into the gully to join them. Henry's teeth were chattering like a machine gun, but Toad was fine. Apparently that pup was warming him up.

"Why don't you let the dog warm you up too?" I asked Henry.

"B-b-because it's a d-d-dog… and I'm a p-p-person. I need something hot that's not a dog. Preferably something like h-h-hot c-c-cocoa. Or hot pancakes. Hot donuts. Hot dogs. Hot t-t-tamales."

Amelia looked worried. "I think something's

terribly wrong with him. He needs a doctor."

"Oh, no, he's fine. This is how he always talks."

"Seriously?"

"Yes, seriously."

"Well, I don't have hot donuts or hot dogs. But I could probably get you guys a hot fire and some hot cocoa. You interested?"

"You kidding?"

I gave my coat to Henry, and we followed Amelia and Miley through the woods. Without snowshoes, it was tough going for Henry and Toad, but slowly and surely, we made it. Through the woods, across another slope of white snow, then back into more trees, and down into a little dip. That's when we came to a small valley with a log cabin at its center.

Amelia skied up to the front porch and took off her skis. She turned around and rang a bell that was hanging from the rafters. "You all plan on freezing to death?" she shouted.

The three of us hustled to join her. Henry

and Toad immediately went inside, while I paused to take off my snowshoes. By the time I entered, Amelia had built a fire in the fireplace. Henry was sitting on a rocking chair next to it, while Toad sat on a rug directly in front of it, stroking Miley's fur.

Amelia was at a small, old-looking stove. She was stirring cocoa into a hot pan of milk. It smelled delicious.

The cabin was small, and just one room. Two rocking chairs were arranged beside the fire, with a third, ordinary chair against the wall. A small table had a chess set on it, and a kitchen table was set for two. A ladder led above the kitchen to a loft.

"Nice cabin," I said.

Amelia looked over at me. "Yes, it is nice. Cozy. And it works for me and my folks."

"You said your dad is a mountain man? And your mom's a skier?"

"Yes. Dad's grandfather built this cabin, and when Dad was old enough, he moved out here.

DANIEL KENNEY

Mom was born in Denver, but she came out to Aspen, met my dad, and fell in love. Twice. First with my dad, and then a few years ago when they opened the first ski lift in Aspen, she fell in love with skiing."

Amelia poured hot chocolate into tin cups and brought them over to us on a metal tray. One for Henry, one for Toad, and one for me. I sat in the second rocking chair and took a deep, satisfying sip.

"Thank you," I said. "For everything."

"Don't mention it." Amelia grabbed the chair by the wall and pulled it to the edge of the rug. She looked at Henry.

"April here says you come to Aspen from Denver."

Henry's hands were wrapped around his cup of cocoa, and I gave him one of those looks. He winked at me.

"Sure did."

"And she said you're in town for the world championships next week."

I gave him another one of those looks.

"Yep," he said. "That's why we're here."

Amelia looked at both of us, then stood. "That is really interesting. Really, *really* interesting. In fact, there are two things really interesting about all of this. The first is, the world championships?"

She paced back and forth, then stopped and looked right at me.

"They ended two days ago."

Uh-oh.

"And the second interesting thing is this. I was out this morning, skiing down the mountain, when thirty feet in front of me, what should happen? A girl falls from the sky and lands into four feet of fresh powder. April, that girl was you."

Amelia sat back down.

"Now. How about you tell me what's *really* going on here?"

CHAPTER SEVEN

A VERY IMPORTANT SECRET

Henry stopped drinking his cocoa. He looked at Amelia, then he looked at me. Toad stopping petting Miley. He looked at me too.

And me?

I didn't know what to say. In all the time traveling we'd done, nobody had ever *caught* us. Looking back on it, I wasn't sure why. We'd been lucky, some. But I suppose mostly, people are so busy, they don't always notice what's going on right in front of them.

But Amelia… this mountain girl with the curious blue eyes… she'd noticed.

Maybe it was because she was all alone in the silent snowy wilderness, soaking in God's grandeur.

But there was no way I could explain how I had just instantly appeared in the sky and fell into a snowbank.

I also wasn't sure if I could tell her the truth.

So I said nothing.

"Let's try this again," said Amelia. "A girl falls from the sky right in front of me. The girl has no winter gear on. She doesn't know where her friends are. She has no idea what she's doing in Aspen. Neither do her friends. My guess is she didn't even know she was in Aspen at all. And then there's this book. This *special* book." She paused and looked at each of us in turn. "Listen, I know this mountain better than anybody other than my dad. And you three? You don't belong here. I *also* love books and stories. I love to make up my stories. With all the quiet of the mountains, I make up stories all day long. And I may not know what's so special about that book, but I have a feeling there's a *great* story in here."

She took another sip of her cocoa and smiled.

"So how about you tell it to me?"

"I don't think I can tell you what's going on," I said.

"How come?"

"I think it's against the rules."

"What rules?"

"I don't think I can tell you that."

"Well then. We have a problem."

"Why's that?"

"Because right now, you're in *my* cabin, drinking *my* hot cocoa, and relaxing by *my* fire. And I'm curious about your story. I'm definitely curious. But if you really don't want to tell me, that's your business. I understand."

"Then what's the problem?"

"The problem is my folks—specifically my dad. Like I told you, he's a mountain man. He knows everything about this mountain. He's knows everyone on this mountain. And when he finds out I've brought three strangers into his cabin, *he's* going to want to know your story. And he's going to *insist* that you tell him."

"And if I can't tell him either?"

"He definitely won't understand."

I tapped the side of my hot cocoa. "Henry, what do you think?"

Henry shrugged. "I don't think the world will blow up, if that's what you mean. I mean, I'm a fairly big buffoon, and *I* know all about the book, right?"

"Toad?" I said. "Do you and Miley have an opinion?"

Toad gave the dog a long, considering look. "Miley thinks her owner should know the truth."

I took a deep breath. "Well. Okay then." I turned to Amelia. "For starters, what year is it?"

"Are you joking?"

"I am not. You were right when you said my book was special. In fact, it's so special that without it, I don't know what year it is."

"How can that be?"

"Just tell me what year it is."

"It's 1950."

"And the exact date?"

"February 20, 1950. But how do you not know this? Are you from a cave or something?"

"No, we're not from a cave. We're from… the future."

"The future what?"

"I knew this was going to be hard." I took the book from my pants and showed her the cover. "Remember how I told you this was a book about the history of Colorado?"

"Sure."

"And you just told me it's February 20, 1950."

She nodded.

"So what I do is I flip through the book until I come to February of 1950." I opened the book and found the page. "And that's where I find *this* passage."

I read aloud:

"February thirteenth through eighteenth, 1950. The World Alpine Ski Championships were held in Aspen, Colorado, for the very first time. These were the first ski world championships held outside of Europe."

Amelia gave me a puzzled look. "I'm not following," she said. "This is all information I already knew. I was at the world championships every day. And I just told you they ended two days ago."

"But did you see me write that in my book? Did you see me visit a printer? Do you think they printed a brand new history of Colorado in the last day?"

The puzzled look on Amelia's face wasn't going away. I could tell she was trying to put it together.

She held out her hand. "Let me see for myself."

I hesitated. "Okay. I'll show it to you. But… I'm going to cover up a bunch of stuff."

"Why?"

"Because the stuff I'm going to cover up hasn't happened yet. At least not for you. And if you knew about it, now… that really might screw something up."

I placed my hand below the information about the recent dates, so she couldn't see anything that followed. And as Amelia read the account of the world championships, her expression grew more and more confused.

When she was done, I closed the book. "When you said this book was special…" I said. "Well, it's very, *very* special. This book lets us travel through time."

Amelia's mouth fell open. "Through time? Like… like a time machine?"

"Exactly like a time machine."

"I don't understand. How is that even possible?"

"Honestly, we don't understand either, and we don't know how it's possible. All we can tell you is our story. But there's one condition. You can't tell anybody, and I mean *any*body, what we tell you."

Amelia shrugged. "Okay."

And so we told her. We told her about the night at the museum and the old book our father had found. We told her how he opened it up and the light came out and everything shook and how then he was gone. We told her how it all happened again when I opened the book. And then we told her everything else.

"So now this book sends you back through history so you can find all the puzzle pieces… and when you've found them all, you think it will let you be with your dad again?"

"That's our hope. After Colorado, we think there's only one state left. And then, hopefully, we can get our dad and travel back to New York, in the future."

"That's the most incredible thing I've ever

heard," Amelia said. She chewed on her lip for a moment. "Isn't it scary?"

"Sure. But what option do we have? Toad and I would do anything to save our dad and get back home."

Amelia was about to say something else when a rumble sounded outside the cabin. It was like distant thunder.

Amelia's eyes grew big. "Shhh," she said, holding up a hand. "Listen."

She craned her neck as if to listen more carefully.

Miley sprang up from in front of the fire and started to bark. Toad gave me a worried look.

The noise grew louder. Now it didn't sound so much like thunder, but like a train getting closer.

Amelia leapt to her feet and yelled:

"*Avalanche!*"

COLORADO

CHAPTER EIGHT

AVALANCHE!

Amelia and Miley ran to the window, and the rest of us followed. We watched together as snow cascaded through the forest and trees with violent speed, while the little cabin shook like we were having an earthquake.

It was incredible. Like watching the powerful waves of an ocean of snow roll down the mountain.

Thirty seconds later, the shaking stopped, and the mountain grew quiet.

"Is that it?"

"For now!" Amelia ran to a big closet next

to the kitchen. She threw open the doors and started throwing out boots and coats and hats and gloves.

"What's all this for?" Henry asked.

"For you three. We need to gear up."

"I don't know much about avalanches," said Henry. "Okay, I don't know *anything* about avalanches… I mean, I know a lot about molten lava cakes and—"

"Henry!" I snapped. "What's your point?"

"Isn't it dangerous to be outside right after an avalanche?" he asked.

"In case there's another avalanche?" said Amelia. "Yeah, it is."

"Then why do you want to go out there?" Toad said.

"I don't *want* to. But my parents went out to check dad's traps earlier this morning. That means they're out there somewhere. And no matter how well you know these mountains, there's only so much you can do against thousands of tons of snow."

"Which means?" asked Henry.

"Which means they might be in trouble," said Amelia. "I'm a lot like you, and I'd do anything to save my parents and get back home. I have to make sure they're okay."

Amelia looked at me, her curiously blue eyes suddenly fierce. "And I need your help."

We scrambled to get the gear on. Out on the porch, Amelia helped Henry and Toad with two extra pairs of snowshoes while I put on the ones from before. She gave us each a pair of ski poles, stepped into her skis, and we were off, with Miley running alongside.

By now, I was getting a hang of the snowshoes, and it wasn't that hard for Henry either. The snowshoes were awfully big on Toad, and it was difficult for his short little legs to move very fast in the deep snow, but soon enough, we made it to the edge of the forest.

It was incredible—somehow the avalanche had spared the part of the mountain where the cabin was, but here, just a couple hundred yards away, snow was piled up in in a wholly unnatural way, like the way snowplows pile up snow on the edges of parking lots. That made the going tougher and slower—and frankly, I had no idea how Amelia expected to find anybody out here.

"You're sure they're out here?" I asked.

She looked at me, her face full of worry. "No. But I can't stay back in the cabin and just *hope* they're okay. I'm pretty familiar with the route they take each morning, so maybe we'll get lucky."

We kept going. Through the woods, over freshly laid mountains of avalanched snow. Occasionally, Amelia would yell for her parents. Her voice traveled for only a bit before being swallowed up by the trees and the stillness of it all.

We'd probably been gone from the cabin for an hour when I noticed Amelia's voice had begun to change. There was a fear in it I hadn't heard before.

"We're going to find them," I said.

All Amelia could do was go faster.

Thankfully, Toad was finally getting the hang of the snowshoes, so he wasn't too far behind, and Henry must have sensed the seriousness of it all, because I hadn't heard him mention hot dogs or hot tamales for a long time.

When we exited the woods on the opposite side, we were on a very different-looking part of the mountain. Here there were rocky faces and cliffs and not many trees at all. I came up alongside Amelia as she looked out at the vastness and starkness of the mountainside.

"Who am I kidding?" she said. "They could be anywhere."

"Then we keep looking," I said.

Henry came up on the other side of Amelia. "That's right. We keep looking."

Amelia yelled once more for her parents, and the rest of us joined in. Even Miley barked along with us. Here, our voices seemed to echo more and get swallowed up less.

Then Toad yelled from behind us. "Stop!"

We all stopped and turned around.

"Do you hear that?" he asked.

We stopped and listened, spinning around, trying to figure out from what direction the noise was coming from.

But Toad pointed to the ground. "No, it's coming from down there."

Amelia skied toward Toad, dropped to the ground, put her ear to the snow, and listened. And then her eyes widened and her mouth curved into a smile. She started yelling.

"Mom! Dad! Mom! Dad!"

I could hear their answer, but only faintly— from beneath the snow.

Amelia took her ski poles and started digging straight into the snow at that spot. The three of us joined her, digging like mad.

"It's me! Amelia!" she shouted into the snow. "And we're coming for you!"

Within ten minutes we'd created a hole about as wide as a frisbee and as deep as one of our ski poles. But it was hard to dig any further, because we could only get as far as Henry's arms could reach.

"We need to make the hole wider," I said. "Then one of us can get down there and keep digging."

It took us another ten minutes to widen the hole enough for Amelia to get into it. She worked feverishly, yelling down to her parents as she dug. And with each passing minute their voices got stronger, telling us that we were getting close.

"How on Earth did they survive down there?" I asked.

"My folks are experienced—they probably hid under a cliff or a rocky cave," Amelia said. "They've got some air. I just don't know how much."

Ten minutes later, Amelia looked up.

"Okay, the snow's getting tender here. Help me up."

Henry and I grabbed her by the arms and

pulled her up. She took out her rope, walked it around the upslope side of the nearest boulder, then walked it back around the other side.

"Okay, Henry, I'm going to need your strength."

Henry puffed out his chest. "For the record, you are the first person in history to suggest I have strength."

"Seriously?" said Amelia. "I could have sworn you were a mountain man."

Henry smiled. "So *you* see it too?"

Amelia winked at me. "Definitely, Henry." She tied one end of the rope around Henry's waist, and tied the other end around one of her ski poles. Then she put Toad in front of Henry, holding on to the rope with two hands. "When the time is right, I need the two of you to pull on this rope with everything you've got."

Then, carrying the ski pole tied to the rope, she lowered herself back into the hole and started to jab the end of the pole into the snow. When she got another foot deeper, the snow around her feet started to give way. She wedged her boots into the side walls of the hole, then heaved the pole downwards as hard as she could.

And she broke through.

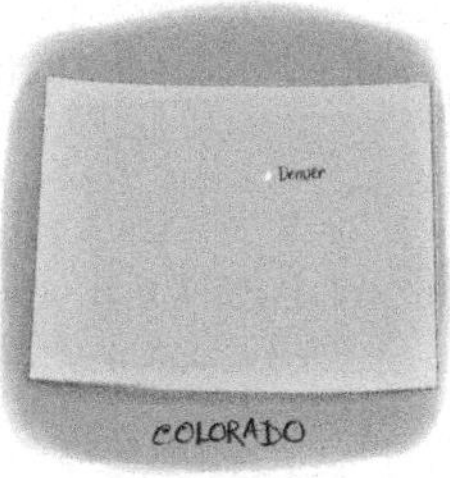
Denver
COLORADO

Chapter Nine

Meet The Parents

Amelia scrambled up the side of the hole, and I pulled her up the rest of the way. Then she joined me on her belly and looked over the edge of the hole. About fifteen feet of rope had fallen into the hole where she had dropped the ski pole through.

"Mom! Dad! Can you hear me?"

That tiny hole was like a well cut into the middle of a snow mountain. And as we stared at it, we saw a hand.

"Amelia!" her father called up. "I've got the rope, honey. I'll tie your mom off first."

"Okay, Dad. Tug it hard when you need us to start pulling."

Amelia looked at her little pup. "Miley, you stay here and watch over Mom." Then she turned to me. "You're coming with me. Those boys are going to need our help."

We ran to join the boys. I grabbed the rope in front of Toad, and Amelia grabbed in front of me. Just then, we felt a big tug on the rope.

Amelia yelled, "Pull!"

We pulled with every bit of strength we had, and the rope started to move. At first, it moved only a little. We strained against the rope and it bent against the rock. But then, steadily, the rope began to inch along, and we began to move backwards. And then, after a minute or so, the rope was suddenly weightless, and we heard a woman's voice yelling, "Amelia!"

Amelia let go of the rope and took off around the boulder. We followed her to see her jumping into the arms of her mother while Miley jumped up and pawed at them both.

Amelia's mother had dark hair and was taller, but otherwise they could have been twins.

After they shared a warm hug, Amelia's mother pulled back. "How about we get your father out of there?"

The two of them dropped the ski pole and rope back down the hole, and then we all went back around the boulder to pull on the other end. This time, Amelia's mother stood behind Henry, and when we felt Amelia's dad tug on the rope, we all pulled together.

Again, slowly but steadily, the rope inched along. And again, the load went suddenly light.

A man's husky voice called out, "I'm out!"

Amelia took off. This time we found her wrapped around her father's neck, holding him tight. He let her go, then knelt down in front of her. His face and his beard were covered in snow, and he was holding Amelia by her shoulders.

"That was foolish of you to come looking for us."

"I know, but—"

"I didn't finish. It was foolish, but I'm awfully glad you did it. I'm proud of you, Amelia. You saved our lives."

"Does that mean we can go into town tomorrow and buy a big bag of candy?"

He laughed. "Is that what our lives are worth? A big bag of candy? Well, darling, under the circumstances, I think that can be arranged."

He gave her another hug, then stood and looked over at the rest of us.

"I thank all of you for your help, but I must confess, I'm at a loss. Who are you?"

"I'm April," I said. "This is my little brother Toad, and this is our friend Henry."

"Where are you from?"

"New York."

"New York? That's a long way. Were you in town for the world championships?"

"It's complicated."

He gave me a funny look. "Well, maybe we can warm up at the cabin and you can tell us all about it."

He took off his backpack and took out his skis. He handed one set to his wife and put one set on himself. "Oh, I almost forgot. Amelia, I found something unusual when we were stuck down there." He reached into his pocket, then pulled out his gloved hand and opened it. "It's some kind of crystal. I've never seen anything like it before."

Amelia grabbed the crystal and held it up toward me with a smile. "Is there any chance *this* is what you are looking for?"

"Yes, I think it is."

"Wait, you've been *looking* for that?" said Amelia's mom.

"Is it part of the complicated story you're going to tell us?" asked Amelia's dad.

I shrugged. "I guess so."

"Well, this must be some kind of a story," he

said. "Now let's get going before my face falls off."

That's when we heard the rumble. And along with it, the ground beneath us began to shake.

"Avalanche!" Amelia's dad yelled. "We need to get down the mountain fast!"

"Dad!" Amelia yelled. "All they've got is snowshoes. They'll never make it in time!"

The rumble and the shaking got worse. The snow was coming. "They've got to jump on our backs," said Amelia's dad. "Honey, we've got to go!"

But I knew that would never work. We were too heavy. We'd slow them down, and then *they'd* never make it down the mountain in time. The snow was just too fast.

"No, you guys save yourselves," I said. "We have another way out."

"You can't do anything against thousands of tons of mountain snow," said Amelia's mom.

"It's part of the complicated story."

I pulled the book out and held the crystal in my other hand.

Amelia looked at the snow coming down the mountain. And then at me. There was fear in her eyes.

"Amelia," I said, "it was a pleasure knowing you. Remember, nobody can ever know this secret. Now go!"

Amelia mouthed the words "thank you," and then she and her parents raced down the mountain.

I looked up the slope. The snow was coming right at us. Then I looked down the slope. Amelia and her parents had stopped to look back.

There was only one thing left to do.

"Ready, boys?"

I slammed the puzzle piece into the book.

The book glowed, and light shot out like a giant camera flash. Now everything was *really* shaking. I didn't know if it was from the book or the snow roaring down the mountain.

Henry and Toad stuck their hands into the book.

And just as the ocean of snow was upon us… everything froze.

The ferocious snowy scene before us, avalanche and all, folded back on itself like the page of a book.

And we began to fall.

I fell and I fell and I fell.

Then suddenly, I landed.

My eyes were closed. I was on top of something like a diving board. It was bouncing up and down, and my hands were wrapped around it.

I opened my eyes. Thirty feet below me was water. Dark, raging, rolling water.

Someone yelled behind me. "It's a girl, Captain! There's a *girl* on the plank!"

Plank?

I got to my feet—and realized that was a terrible mistake. I really was on something like a diving board, except instead of extending over a pool, it was over a dark and raging sea. And in standing up, I almost lost my balance. Crouching once more to steady myself, I turned around and stood—more slowly this time.

In front of me was a man wearing a black hat

and an eye patch, and behind him was a crew of rough-looking men wearing old-timey clothes. They were all standing on a ship. An old wooden ship. A black flag with a white skull and crossbones flew from the mast.

"You're… *pirates*?" I said.

"Aye, missy, and this is our ship. And you're on it. Or more to the point, you're on the plank. Now why would that be?"

I started to shake.

And then the man next to the captain pointed at something at my feet. "Captain. She's got a book."

Book?

I spun around and looked down. The book was right there, on the plank. I reached down to grab it.

But just at that moment, the ship rocked horribly. I grabbed both sides of the plank and held on.

The book wasn't so lucky.

I watched in slow motion as the book fell

from the plank and tumbled into the sea below.

"*No!*" I screamed.

I turned around, panicking.

"We found two more stowaways, Captain!"

A fat pirate appeared behind the others. He was holding Henry and Toad by the scruffs of their necks and was pushing them toward the captain.

"Henry, Toad!" I yelled. "Are you okay?"

Henry wrinkled his nose. "As long as Sailor Smells-A-Lot lets go of us, then yes, we should be fine."

I looked once more down to the ocean below. To my amazement, the book was still there! It was floating on the surface. But with the way the waves were rolling over each other, I knew it wouldn't be afloat for long.

I looked back at Henry, then at Toad. I gave Toad a weak smile. He smiled back.

Then I did the only thing I could do.

I jumped.

Join *April, Henry,* and *Toad* on their
continuing adventures in

The History Mystery Kids Book #5

"Sabotage in South Carolina!"

Can you help me spread the word about
THE HISTORY MYSTERY KIDS?

If you enjoyed reading about April, Toad, and Henry's adventures, I would be honored if you asked a parent to help you write a short review about my Book on Amazon.com or Goodreads.

Reviews help other readers find my books, and I want to introduce THE HISTORY MYSTERY KIDS to as many readers as possible. Thank you so much for your help!

~ Daniel Kenney

BOOKS BY DANIEL KENNEY
FOR YOUNG READERS

The History Mystery Kids Series of
Time Travel Adventures

The Math Inspectors Series of Mysteries

The Science Inspectors Series of Mysteries

The Big Life of Remi Muldoon
Illustrated Adventure Series

Pirate Ninja Humorous Adventure Series

The Beef Jerky Gang Middle Grade Novel

Katie Plumb & The Pendleton Gang
Middle Grade Novel

Teenage Treasure Hunter Middle Grade Novel

*Search for Daniel Kenney on Amazon
to find all of his books for young readers.*

ABOUT THE AUTHOR
DANIEL KENNEY

Daniel Kenney is the bestselling children's author behind the hit detective series The Math Inspectors and The Science Inspectors. He is also the author of The Big Life of Remi Muldoon, Pirate Ninja, The Beef Jerky Gang, Katie Plumb & The Pendleton Gang, Teenage Treasure Hunter and other funny books for smart and adventurous kids. Daniel and his wife live in Nebraska with lots of big kids and one very small dog. When those kids aren't driving him nuts, he is busy writing books, drawing pictures, cheering on the Benedictine Ravens, and learning to play the fiddle.

Made in the USA
Las Vegas, NV
03 December 2021

35980765R00080